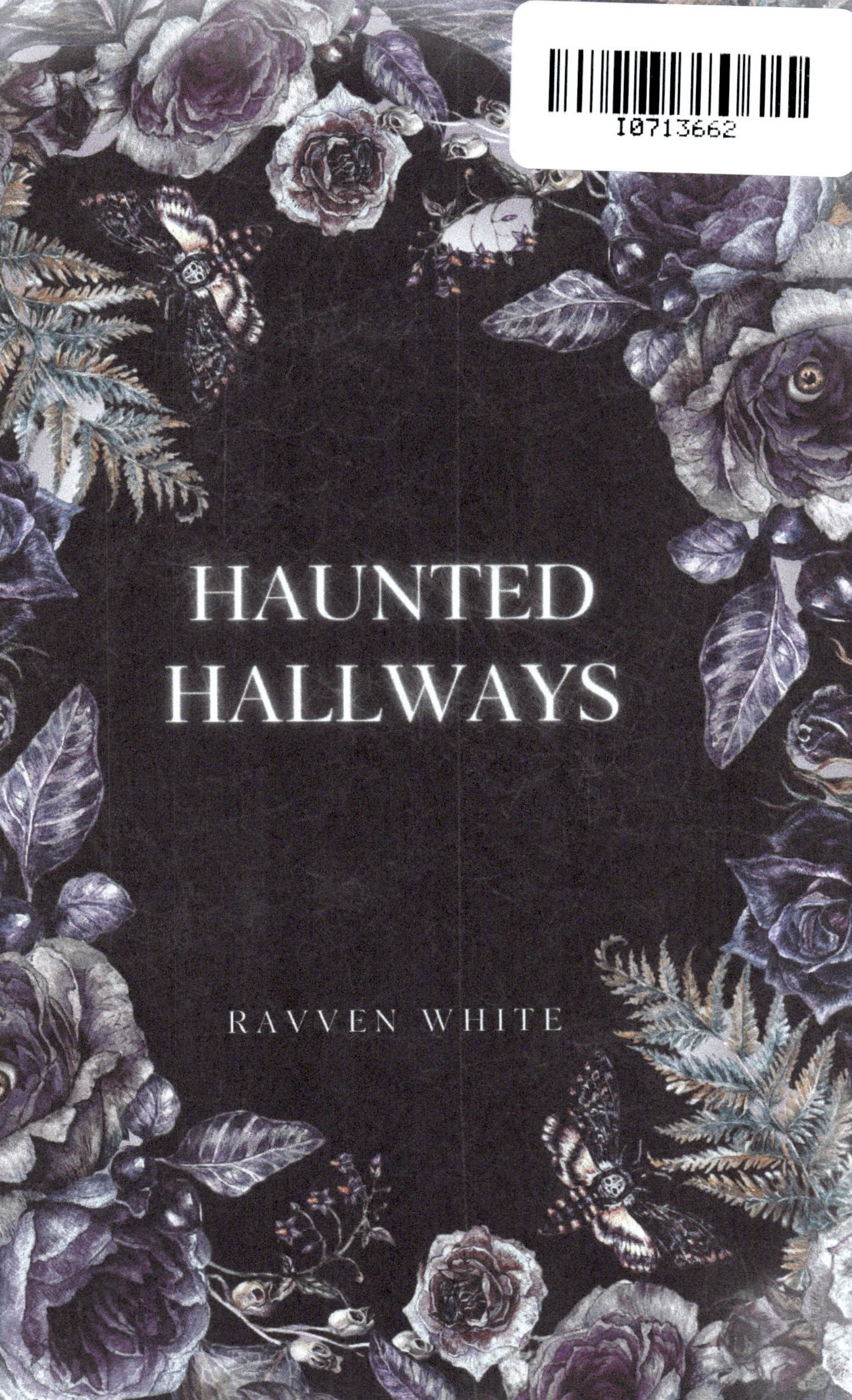
HAUNTED
HALLWAYS
RAVVEN WHITE

Curious Corvid
PUBLISHING

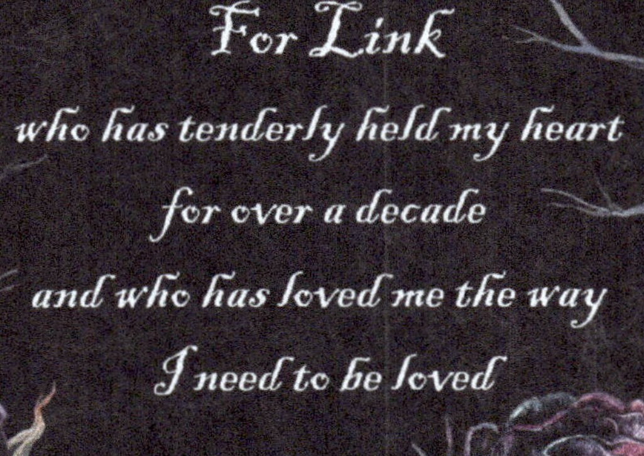

For Link

who has tenderly held my heart

for over a decade

and who has loved me the way

I need to be loved

Contents

The Battlement

The Dungeon

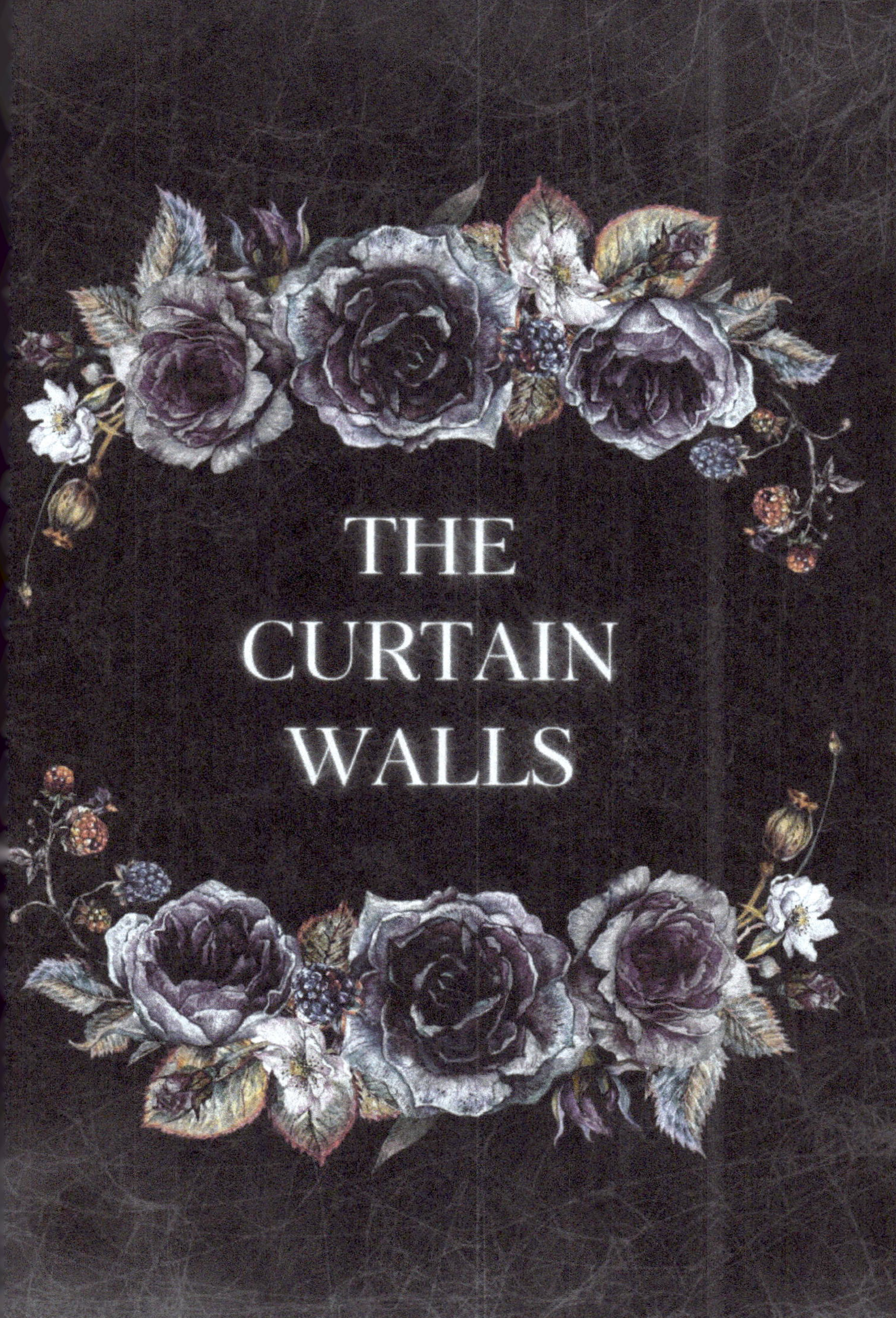

THE CURTAIN WALLS

January 15th

Here it is, the day I am to be wed to my heart of hearts! Truthfully, I would be lying if I said I was not afraid. I do not know him as well as I would like to. Mother says I know all that I need to and I have filled my head with far too many fairy tales and romance novels. Perhaps she is right but I see no harm in dreaming of a Prince Charming and a castle in the sky... He is rather reserved. I've only met him but a handful of times and he seemed..distant. Aloof? My cousins say that is masculinity and it means he will be a good leader of our home. I will miss my cousins. I am used to laughter and sunshine and constant companionship. He lives far away and his home is an old family castle. It's very quiet and empty. Quite large for such few people as even the servants are scarce. I hope I shall not lose myself among the keeps and hallways. I'm sure he would allow me guests, especially if it is my own family.

At least he is handsome. That cannot be denied. He is tall, with sun-kissed skin and eyes that hold the richness of a deep and plentiful pine forest. I remained composed the first time that I saw him but I admit, inside I was melting from his gaze. I wonder if he will want many children...

I...I am sure I can make him love me. Father used to tell me that I make any who see me fall desperately in love. Let us hope that holds true, even now. I miss Father. I wish he was here for this day

childish

I've seen you glance me from the corner of your eye

You say you're not interested but I know you lie.

This is the time for lovers, both momentary and forever,

The air thick with lust and longing, courting one another.

But would you have me as I am, or have you pre-designed

What I look and sound like, am I flesh without the mind?

Or would you have the whole of me: heart and soul and body?

You cannot change once you decide, so choose desire wisely.

When I was a child, my mother told me

That someday I would make a man very happy.

I would love him more than he loved me

But it would be okay because

Women are meant to be *lovers*

And Men are meant to be *consumers*

And I see now for I *am* consumed,

Thoughts and longings and desires

Echoing in the chambers of a wanton heart.

But

How empty to be a lover unconsumed themselves,

And I remembered that though my mother told me

I would someday make a man very happy

She neglected to mention

If I would be happy, too.

𝕴t is with resolution that we fall in love,

For love is a choice, a bargain, a contract

A binding of two lonely hearts that decide

"You are for me and I am for you."

- oh how quickly we forget ourselves -

In our hearts we cling to the concept

Of a love eternal and unending,

A falling that we cannot control,

A burning that threatens the world

And all of existence, on behalf of this person

Who has taken us mind, body, and soul.

But love is a choice.

We *choose* to stay.

We *choose* to overlook.

We *choose* to overcome.

We *choose* to forgive.

We *choose* each other, ideally.

Love is a choice.

So when I say that I love you,

I love you with all of my being,

I surrender my heart and my comfort

To whatever storms may come,

I forfeit the future that could have been

The lovers that might have been,

The person I would have become

And instead, I choose *you*.

I choose you

And I choose love

And I hope and pray

That it will be enough.

𝔍

Wonder

Will you stay?

Under the moon,

Flirting with the stars,

We could be everything.

Star gazing lovers lost in

A reverie, so sweetly. Hold me.

Hold me like you love me. *Like you could.*

And tomorrow when the sun rises

We will be only as shadows.

I will think of you fondly

And if we are lucky

Our shadows will merge.

You will hold me,

I'll hold you

Beneath

Stars.

And I will love you

Even as the last breath leaves me

Even as my blood grows cold inside me

And even then,

In the twilight haze of grief

I will love you.

I will hold you in the glow of starlight,

In the comfort of a dark night.

When the day calls for me to leave you,

Know I have loved you

With every fiber of my being,

A love transcending eternity.

And I will have no shame in saying

I loved you.

   I loved you.

     I loved.

I don't require much

In terms of love:

Just some time

And some quiet—

Perhaps hand holding…

But mostly time.

And isn't time

As fleeting

As love?

And if you find it in yourself

To spare some time

And sit awhile with me,

I will grow you wildflowers

Who whisper sweet nothings,

Sweet nothings

That mean everything.

THE
MOAT

March 1st

It has been nearly two moon cycles since I first arrived at my new home. I wish I could describe my passing days as wedded bliss, but nothing could be further from the truth... the day itself was the most beautiful experience I have ever witnessed. I was dressed in ivory lace and satin, decorated in white roses and narcissus. My intended greeted me at the altar in his royal colors of midnight blue and gold, the sun embroidered across his chest. We took our vows before our family and before the gods as a slight mist descended on the grounds, covering us in rainbows and shimmering stars. The celebrations were joyous, we danced and drank and celebrated...

When the evening drew close and we were paraded to our chambers, I knew the time had come for the consummation of our celebration. My heart beat furiously and as I thought of his lips tracing my flesh, I felt the heat and desire I have only read about. The doors closed and I stood still, waiting, ready to shed my satin and deliver my most sacred gift.

But all my preconceived ideas vanished as my beloved turned upon me, forcing me on the bed muttering, "let's get this over with."

There were no soft words or tongue or touch. Just pain and astonishment that turned to tears and disappointment. In a few moments, it was over. And then he left.

And I have not seen him since.

There are more ways to be intimate

Than by flesh of the body,

- would you like to know me? -

I house secrets and travesty.

During our innermost moment

I will confess I am not good enough

- I couldn't stop the things I should've -

Just a shadow of who I could have...

This body is so temporary

But scars on souls last forever

- Haunted whispers that sever -

Shall I let you know me now...or never?

If I were drowning,

Would you save me?

Or would you watch

And count the choking bubbles

Until you were free?

I could teach you how to love me.

I could teach you how to touch me.

- I am lonely -

I would do almost *anything*

To make you notice me.

Within me ripples a solitude

I have never asked to know

As I was made for the sunlight

Rather than the moon's eternal glow.

I was made for laughing and dancing

For love, for life, for thrills

But all I have now is a solitude

And a sadness that slowly kills.

Have you heard the whispering

Lurking within the walls?

They warned me to not go out at night,

To avoid the empty halls.

Perhaps it is simply the loneliness--

But perhaps it is something more;

I hear the calls at midnight hours

And the knocks upon my door.

But oh, what a mystery grief is,

How it can twist and morph and grow.

It leaves lesions all over the body

That show in the cracks of your soul.

And I wonder if all that does linger

When the silence descends in the night,

Is not a ghost that is haunting,

But a heartbroken and haunted wife?

THE
GATE

July 16th

It is so suffocating and not just due to the heat. I do not know what it is about this castle. It feels so empty and yet...so full. As if there are a hundred souls walking through it's ruins. Sometimes I hear whispers or laughing. At night I wake to the sounds of footsteps and knocking. I used to think it was Him coming to me, finally. Ready to embrace me.

But no one is ever there. My mother hushes me when I talk about the whispers. She says it is the loneliness and that I must care for my solitude. I think she is more afraid of my breaking this arrangement and losing access to His family wealth.

I do not wish to be alone.

I attempted to make friends with one of the maids. She has a lovely smile and seems so full of life. But she shied away from me when I approached her. I think she is afraid of something, though she did tell me something rather strange.

"Do not walk these hallways alone. Especially at night."

I do not know how I should walk the hallways not alone as I have no one, and not even she will stay.

I just want Him to love me. We could be happy.

Maybe I shall surprise Him.

Yes I think He would like that.

July 18th

I saw Him I saw Him with her. I don't even know her who
is she why does she think she can have him??? And Him,
He was inside her making her sweat and scream and I am
here I am right here I am here I am here I am here I
am here .

Why doesn't he love me? Why doesn't anyone see me?
And the whispers go on and on and they are the only
companionship I have and they aren't even real
They're not even real but I am real I am
real I am real I am real

I don't deser ve this I have done nothing but love him and
this is how he repays me this is what I get for waiting and
waiting and waiting . .

And walking these hallways over and over and over and over
and whispers just whispers all the time everywhere not even

whispers anymore, screams screams screams that's how
I found them, the screams led me to them because
the screams love me. The whispers love me. Love me
love me love me I deserve it

He is Mine.

There is no such torture as a heart on the line—

Whispers of love over half drunk bottles of wine.

The "could be" the "would be" the "what does it mean?"

As hopes quell themselves and patience grows lean.

No such pain as one heart in love and one not

With potential promise painfully blossoming on.

One must wonder how much time one can take

As love longs to linger when the heart waits.

I thought I'd have more time

As I watched you walk on by.

I did not know this kiss

Was actually "*Goodbye*".

Silence is violent

In empty beds, in busy heads

(Numbness left to hold you)

With coldness there to hold you

The death of a love.

He is not in love with me

Though I'm in love with him…

This is not how I thought 'twould be

But it's just starting to begin

Maybe now or never

Does it really matter?

I know that I'm in love with him

And love can make it better.

He is mine, He is MINE, MINE MINE MINE MINE MINE MINE

MINE

THE
KEEP

October ??

He finally came to me. He said he was sorry, that He had known her and loved her before I was brought into His life, that our marriage was just a power move.

He said He thought I knew.

I told Him I did not want to know her name, that she musn't be allowed back, that He cannot see her that He must love me and only me because He is mine, mine, He is mine, He is mine mine mine mine!!!!!!!

He said he could not love me. I told him to try or I would... I would do something terrible. I told him that I know everything that there is nothing that can save him because the whispers know and they tell me things.

He looked scared. I am glad.

I am lonely. I will make him love me.

October ??

It did not last. He is a liar.

I caught her sneaking through the hallways. The screams helped me find her, and she was screaming too, she was coated and covered in blood She deserved it!

I had to take so many showers to get the blood off of me after she got it all over me stupid fucking bitch but shes dead now, she's dead now, the screaming killed her, the whispers, the shadows took her.

I wonder if she'll be a whisper now, too?

Am I whisper?

I joined your kingdom in the clouds,

I questioned not your intentions.

Through pain and suffering I would know

That love was just a mask you were wearing.

Perhaps I should apologize

For all the deeds I've done

But you should not blame a woman

Forced to stay when I wanted to run.

For though my body is a temple

Far too few will see it that way

I will be forced to make concessions

Then shamed for giving it all away

I will be lied to and I'll be burdened

With traumas that are not my own

With hands that touch and hold me

Even when I ask to be alone.

I'll be demanded of and then forgotten

Passed over in love and rewards

Forced to compensate when life is heavy

By whatever means I can afford.

I'll bear you children from my womb

And warm your pillows and your bed

I'll make you meals and wash your clothes

While I wish that you were dead.

        I'll wear a smile and fresh clean dress

           And mop and cook and clean

          I'll tell the world of happiness

        And cover the bruises when you're mean.

And sometime when you're not looking

I'll sharpen the butcher knife

And out I'll gouge your wandering eyes

That should've been watching his loving wife.

        And then I will carve up your body

        And drain your blood into the tub

       Since you wanted me to always be pretty

        You'll make the perfect sugar scrub.

Then I'll bury you deep in the garden

And no one will ever know

I'll cry that you ran off one day

And you left me all to my own.

But your teeth I think I will keep them

And your eyes, of course, my dear

For each time that I gaze upon them

I will see your raw unfiltered fear.

So yes, maybe I should apologize

For all of the deeds I have done.

But really, its just self-preservation

Who cares if I also have fun?

Because no one will care when he hits me

Or cheats, or screams, or rapes.

Nobody cares when a wife is betrayed

Since we all made the forced choice to stay.

55

Shhhh

I have been slumbering

And now begins awakening—

I know you thought that I was dead,

But now is the time for reckoning.

I've returned for blood and vengeance,

And I have no use for penance.

You left dead flowers at my door

As if you sought forgiveness.

It's too late for your apology,

You may run but you will never flee—

I am rage incarnate upon this earth

And I have all of your eternity.

And once upon a time,

I cared more than I ought to.
I suppose that we all do
When it comes to matters of the heart.

But hearts, they come apart
If you tear them hard enough

Chewy, juicy vessels
Rotten to its very core.

Shed the skin

You wear each day—

Behind your mask

Sits all I crave.

At night I wander through the halls,

Only to wake and wander more

My eyes are bound by the wish to dream

Though I dream not as before.

And my soul continues my heart to stake—

So goes the Ballad of Heartbreak.

It's sharp and sweet and full of pain

And hope will fly between the strains

To mend the bridge life tried to take—

So goes the Ballad of Heartbreak…

I know you're there

Hiding at the corner,

Reflecting in the mirror,

I would think me crazy

A figure soft and hazy

Barely there and gone

Never close but never farther.

Never close but never farther

But somehow you feel nearer

When the witching hour enters

And I feel your cold breath in my dreams.

Noone sees you

Floating in the background

Projecting to the foreground

Cold spots in the hallways

And lights that flicker always

Toys and trinkets gone

While whispered echoes hang around.

While whispered echoes hang around,

I chance glance your twisted frown

Morph from a smile upside down

And mouth:

'Things are never as they seem'...

I walk through haunted hallways

Echoing in disrepair,

At home with ghosts and spirits

Who no longer hold a care.

They believe they can scare me—

Flickering lights, hollow screams.

They jiggle doors and move things,

Make me question what I've seen.

But I was born in darkness

And of it, I'm unafraid.

A child trapped in sadness,

A blood sacrifice I've paid.

And ghosts, they are far kinder

Than humans have ever been.

They have no need to use me

Nor do they judge my sins.

I rather like their faces

Pitted eyes that sometimes glow.

Their whispers lull me softly,

For at least I'm not alone...

Sometimes I cannot tell what's real

Left to myself to numb the pain,

I sleep and then I walk again.

I sleep, I walk, I sleep, I walk,

And then I wake from deadened dreams

I look for life in stones and mortar,

Tracing pathways in wilting gardens,

Leaving blood trails from bitten fingers,

And so I linger in cavernous silence

I sleep.

      I walk.

         I sleep.

            I walk.

               I wake.

I close my eyes and drift into an uneasy sleep.

Images dance in random sequence

- *how many secrets that you keep* -

Forgetful fingers drumming frequence

Eyes open, but not awake, not living

Eyes close, blinking through static hollows

- *what is it that follows, breathing* -

Rage fueled lungs relax into shallow.

In this phantasmagoria of unending daydream,

If I am awake, am I living? If not, am I dead?

- *are you lucid while you're dreaming* -

Lost in a labyrinth birthed from your head.

Dreaming? Sleeping? Wide awake?

My days are numbered, so who's to say?

I saw the signs too late,

Caught up in your love affair—

The way your hands stroked my hair

As you whispered sweet nothings

That I thought meant something.

Oh, but you were like absinthe

Consumed undiluted,

So drunk off your presence

While deceptively poisoned

And now I fear I will never see clearly

Consumed by hallucinations

That you actually loved me.

THE
BATTLEMENT

November

I know He looks for her. He looks so sad and lonely, just like me, when I look in the mirrors framing the hallways.

He came to me in grief, not knowing I held her in her final moments, .that I breathed her last breath. In desperation He took me and we became one, His breath was my breath, His hands my hands, wrapped around each other's throats, gasping and writhing as He cried out.

But He called her name. hers. her vile putrid name that I did not want to know!

I cast Him out, naked and distraught, I banished Him to the hallways and I told Him where he could find His true one and only, rotting in the catacombs below the castle.

I do not know what overcame me but I feel so strong now. I know what I must do.

November

He looked for her but of course she wasn't there. He thinks I was just saying angry things to hurt Him. He says there is no love between us and that He knows I had something to do with her disappearance and he's filing for divorce.

I just smiled and listened and reminded Him of something very important;

'Til Death do we part.'

He can do whatever He feels He must but He is mine now, He is mine, He is mine and soon my belly will grow with his seed and He will be reminded why He loves me. And if it doesn't, well then I guess He is right and our love isn't real and he will regret every moment he ever led me to think it was and the whispers will come for him as they did for her and I will watch and wait and bathe in his blood because He is MINE

Murmurs, whispers, in the night

Voices playing round my head

They speak of darkness and delight,

Of rivers bathed in deepest red.

I speak not of these words I hear

Nor of shadows that play on walls

For though these murmurs linger near,

I know they are not here at all…

I bite down hard on my tongue.

Blood seeps and mingles with regret.

Why do I do this?

Suffering in a silence so others thrive.

But it's just a lie.

Or is it?

To tell the truth, I've forgotten it

And I'm fairly certain

I never knew truth to begin with.

I loosen my grip as I slowly

slip—

I

A

M

F

A

L

L

I

N

G

Do not catch me.

I will learn to fly.

Or

I will simply

D

I

E

And for some reason,

I smile.

You treat me as a long dead ghost,

Drinking my love til a withered host.

And still, I linger, won't you please remember?

When the summer was warm before September.

I can feel the sickness sleeping,

Consuming as it dreams.

If I were a vampire or werewolf,

It would be shrouded in mystery.

I can feel the sickness feeding,

From the ache around my bones.

If I were a siren or a banshee,

My screams would not be alone.

I can feel the sickness creeping,

As if my body disconnects.

If I were a ghoul or even a zombie,

I wouldn't need the brain above my neck.

I can feel the sickness growing,

One day it will consume.

If I were monster I would not care,

But I'm just a human, just like you.

I found your diary while you were gone

I found your cloak-and-dagger.

Such things that I had never known

Which caused my breath to stagger.

The words were genuine but read surreal,

Crumpled pages stained with tears.

Who would have thought you have to keep

Things hidden the past twelve years?

I dissected your tome from front to back

Just trying to comprehend,

Bloodstains sometimes smudging black,

Seemed your darkness had no end.

Then I heard you singing in the murky night

And saw moonlight kiss your hair.

Fairy like, long dress of white

And you smiled while standing there.

I dropped your book and forced a scream

But darling, you could not hear.

I hated you for such a read,

For letting me see your fears.

My lungs collapsed, I fell to the ground

Hit my head and could not see.

Then in my bed, sore and unsound,

I woke clutching my diary.

I can feel your heartbeat through the floorboards

      Pulsing up into my veins

And I dance to the song you wrote for me

      Describing me my grave

Sometimes when I stand very still

      I can hear you breathing through the walls

My body moves against my will

      When I chase your sullen call

It's suffocating,

      you're suffocating

           I can barely breathe.

                Drowning me in memories

                      Of a long forgotten
                         nobody

Haunted by an unholy thing:

      Dance, dance while you can

           And don't forget to sing.

I caught it creeping, slowly seeping

Through the bottom floor

As I peered over the staircase

Outside my bedroom door.

It slithered and it whispered

Evil things that shouldn't be

But then it turned and off it ran

After it locked it's eyes with me.

Hello

I'm walking through hallways

Broken and full of holes

Carpets stained in blood

Walls leaking tears,

Molding with repressed fears

I wonder if you know

I'm trespassing in your home

Nightly, daily, weekly.

I'm trying to leave

With boxes of baggage

Stacked up around me.

What is this,

This tightening in my chest?

An unsanctioned sensation

Driving me from rest.

Why do these,

These suspicions seize my mind,

As emotional necrosis

And dread consumes my spine?

Do not speak to me of love

For I have seen what love can do.

I have watched the darkness fast descend

And rend a heart in two.

Do not speak to me of passion

A greater traitor there never was

When affection turns to violence

And passion deals in bloods.

Do not speak to me of romance

Or of *'the one and only one'*

For romance is the first to die

When love is on the run.

Do not speak to me of love

For I have known both love and war,

And if you knew what love was…

You would not ask for more.

THE DUNGEON

December

I feel everything and nothing.

I don't sleep anymore, I just walk and wait. I see them all the time now, everywhere. They don't even try to hide anymore. I wonder if they have always been there.

His family will not let him leave me. I am glad he knows what it feels like now.

After he recovered from his fear, he grew angry that she left him. After all, who would leave him? His anger has grown significantly. He hits me now. Sometimes he does other things. He screams most days and nothing pleases him.

I wonder if he was always this way or of the whispers and screams finally got to him. I asked him if he heard them. He did not answer.

It does not matter anyway.

It will all be over soon. I can feel it in my bones, in the way that my blood boils everytime I am forced to look at him.

My belly is empty and I am grateful.

If he were to die, I would be a very wealthy widow. I would have my castle. And my whispers. I am already used to being alone as even my family has abandoned me. Nobody wants to acknowledge a marriage steeped in infidelity and abuse.

~~I am so sorry Father. I tried to make him love me.~~

But what's done is done. And if no one will help me, I will help myself. They will help me help myself. And the whispers will come for him as they did her.
We will be one even if it is in death.

- I should not be here -

Padded footsteps on cold stones

Naive to believe I'd be alone.

Hushed whispers, hooded cloaks

Are you real or just a ghost?

Candles waver in the night

Adrenaline moves to fight or flight

I realize nothing is as it seems,

Recognizing

my own

blood-curdling

S

C

R

E

A

M

Seemingly unaware of the way

I *wilted*.

You had the nerve to feel jilted

When I left you.

But I will never forget you—

Forever the marker for tainted lovers.

Daunted and haunted

By a prize you cannot have.

In this crumbling castle, lights flicker dimly

As I solemnly ponder what's happened within me.

Such haunting of echoes in hallways unlit—

A dragging and rattling of chains in the attic,

More empty rooms left in ruin, abandoned.

Dreams once so full now shattered and scattered.

Creatures that scurry cloaked in an umbra of darkness,

Bedrooms bedecked in an unspoken promise.

Barefoot and broken, I walk among shadows

Hounded by grief and the heartache that follows…

Save me from this nightmare,

Before I go insane.

It beckons and it calls me,

From beyond the earthly plane

It lies in wait for me to sleep,

And crawls upon my bed,

Grabs my heart between its claws,

And squeezes it til dead...

Don't you tell a single lie

I will know if you do.

And if you lie, well then I
Will see

      if your blood

                  runs

                         blue…

I can hear your voice

You're crying out, you're screaming.

I can hear your fists still pounding.

I think they might be bleeding.

You've got no choice.

I can hear your heart.

Its pumping hard, it's gushing.

I can feel your veins still throbbing.

I think they're close to bursting.

Tell me does it hurt?

beat..

      beat..

  beat..

            it..

    wasn't..   me

..it was   you..

beat..

           beat..

                beat..

See, truth is, I strive to forgetfully forgive you for something I don't understand.

A fault you fathered when you abandoned the world inside your hand.

A sigh, a song, a something—hidden hallucination,

Your fascinating figures that denied investigation.

So deceivingly delightful with a smile, thick as poison...

See, truth is, without your innocent inviolate quaking to your tune,

You're a nothing and a no one disdainfully deserted by the bloom.

A cough, a click, a whisper—voiceless validation

As you struggle to make the claim of dismayed desperation.

How long until you realize you built your very prison?

About who and what I am.

Of beauty and of grace,

And how you want to hold my hand.

You fed me sugar sweetness

But my body ached for more

And now, my dear, I've twisted

Fully rotten to the core.

Hello?

Shadows dart across my face

Distorting what you see

- is this really me? -

Stop. What did you say?

I turn to face you

- have I gone mad? -

Who am I talking to?

Solid stones whisper trauma

My fingers trace mortar

- have I built a wall or prison? -

Keys of comfort jangle from my waist

I smile at the lack of door

- what have I done? -

Blood kissed footsteps

Haunt forgotten hallways

- did I try to run? -

Locked in a tower, remembering

- I've been here before -

Is this a dream?

Is this a nightmare?

- why do I suddenly care? -

I woke from a slumber I could not remember

Eyes opened as if I had just closed them

I would not say that I suffered, simply slumbered.

I try to recall my name, slipping down the drain

Just barely caressing a forgotten remembering

I smile contentedly,

Understanding I have met the end of me.

And here I will lay bare

All the thoughts that have consumed me:

If he does not love me,

He will not have me.

Not by thought of mind

Nor flesh of body.

But oh, he will *want* me

And oh, how he will *love* me

Because he will see in me

All the things he shall *never* be.

And this twisted love

Will exist only violently

For they have told me,

'When monsters love you,

Monsters hurt you.'

But what he does not know—

Hush now, I will tell you my secret:

He will think me taken

When in truth, I am here to slay him.

Were the skeletons in your past too many for you to hide?

Enlighten my shroud, were you afraid I would find

Your imperfections, impurities throbbing in your veins?

I don't want your blood, it's your heart that I crave.

Keep in mind, darling, you enslaved me this life

I'll have your secluded heart one bleached bone at a time

I'm in love with this sickness vaccinating my soul,

Wrap your chain 'round my neck so we twain will be whole....

If you require a heartbeat to compose you a dirge

Well, love, I am qualified, just grant me your last word

I won't count on your name or demand of your ring

For once I have your heart, well, I'll have everything…

I find the beating of your heart

Captivating

Intoxicating

But disappointing

When I peer closer

Sticky red growing colder

For once it's in my hands

The beating just grows softer.

S o f t e r

S o f t e r

You should have been softer.

"No no NO!

How could you DO this to me?"

My heart is wrenched in agony

Blood squelching on the floor before me

Pooling, sparkling, scented in sadness

"Please, please, PLEASE

DO NOT LEAVE ME TO THIS MADNESS!"

Why, why have I been driven to this?

Tears fall as though an ocean has brimmed inside me

A darkness fast consumes me

"Please." And I am begging as I hold you

"Please do not leave me."

But frozen lips extinguish…

And you leave me to my anguish.

And here I am

Walking hallways unfinished

Bejeweled only in rubies stolen from your veins

Sweet sapphire eyes adorning crimson fingers

Pearly teeth jangling in ruined pockets.

- he is mine and I am his -

Climbing stairs ever upwards

I lose my footing and I reach, I

R

E

A

C

H

for you

And you embrace me as a cold wind

As a dark night

As a piercing scream ripped from bruised lungs

And I fall into you

Into us

Into our murderous and treacherous eternity.

We will never deserve each other

And our whispers that should have been

Heard and answered

Will haunt hallways

And bedrooms

And castles and keeps

While we wait for the

Salvation

Of

Those who know how to speak.

Acknowledgements

Thank you to my hearts and homes both in person and online. You heard my whispers and freed my voice and ultimately saved my life more times than you realize.

You all walked my haunted hallways with me and showed me the way out.

P.S. My husband Link wants you all to know that he is in fact *not* a bad husband or bad man. This is true. He is a cinnamon roll.

Ravven White is a queer gothic poet and novelist. She dabbles in mystery and magic and spends most of her nights reading books or scribbling crazed stories from her pen. The founder of Curious Corvid Publishing, Ravven has a special love for the odd and the unusual and is deeply passionate about indie publishing and fair representation. Ravven lives in a castle by the sea with her husband, daughter, their two hellhounds, and her various familiars. You can usually sense her arrival by a curious flapping of wings.